UNDER THE STAIRS

JEFF GOTTESFELD

SADDLEBACK
EDUCATIONAL PUBLISHING

WH/TE L/GHTNING
BOOKS

BEHIND THE MASK	IGGY	SCRATCH N' SNITCH
BREAK AND ENTER	ON THE RUN	SUMMER CAMP
EMOJI OF DOOM	QWIK CUTTER	THE UNDERDOGS
GRAND SLAM	REBEL	UNDER THE STAIRS

SADDLEBACK
EDUCATIONAL PUBLISHING
www.sdlback.com

ISBN-13: 978-1-68021-143-6
ISBN-10: 1-68021-143-9
eBook: 978-1-63078-541-3

Printed in Malaysia

22 21 20 19 18   2 3 4 5 6

MONSTER FACTS

MONSTER COMES FROM THE LATIN WORD `MONSTRUM`

A LARGE, AQUATIC,
DINOSAUR-LIKE
CREATURE IS SAID
TO LIVE IN A LAKE IN
SCOTLAND CALLED
LOCH NESS

RUMOR HAS IT THIS MONSTER CARRIES AWAY
HUMAN CHILDREN AND EVEN ADULTS!

DIEGO HAS SEEN 8 1/2 MONSTERS BEFORE ...

... BUT ONLY IN HIS NIGHTMARES!

I HOPE WHATEVER IS UNDER THE STAIRS LIKES PB & J!
(MOM BUYS THE CREAMY KIND)

CHAPTER 1

THE CHEST

Paige Tyson grinned. She was with her friends. There was Ava Samuels, her best friend. Diego Jones. And Nate Borman. The kids were on Oak Lane.

At the top of a small hill was a big house. Diego's dad had bought it. The house had been boarded up for a long time. At least since before Paige was born. That was fourteen years ago.

The scary house had belonged to the Benson family. One morning the whole Benson family had been found dead. Most were in their beds. One had been in the basement. They had been stabbed. No one had lived in the house since.

Until now. Diego and his family would move in. Today was the day they got the keys.

"Your dad has a lot of guts," Ava told Diego.

"I don't think it's about guts," Paige said. "Diego's dad is all about making money."

Diego nodded. They were almost at the house. "My dad wants us to live there for a year. He'll fix it up. Then he'll sell it. We'll move again."

"You don't mind?" Nate asked.

"Nah. We've been doing it all my life. You guys know that. As long as we stay in town, it's fine with me."

"As long as you don't die in this place," Ava said.

Diego shook his head. "The cops said an intruder killed the Bensons."

"Maybe," Ava said. "Maybe not. Maybe it was an alien attack."

Paige gave Ava a nudge with her arm. "Chill with your crazy ideas."

Ava was famous for her crazy theories. She believed in ESP. Ghosts. Aliens. Paige thought it was bull. She believed in facts. The cops had said an intruder killed the Bensons. So that's what had happened. No need to give Diego bad dreams.

Paige liked Diego a lot. He was a great artist. They hadn't kissed. Yet. Paige had been in no rush. But she knew the time was coming. School was ending next week. The eighth-grade dance was Monday night. Maybe their first kiss would be there. For the longest time she hadn't been ready. Now she was.

The kids got to the house. The place was big, brown, and old. It had a huge front porch. The porch could be nice if it got cleaned up. There was a moving truck out front. Also a huge pile of junk. The Joneses' minivan too. But no people.

"Where are your folks, Diego? Hey. Maybe they're dead already!" Ava said.

"Ava?" Diego said.

"Yeah?"

"Shut up." Diego started up the stone walk. The kids followed him across the porch. They went through the open door. Inside was a sea of boxes. "Anyone home?" Diego called.

They heard his dad's voice from upstairs. "Hey! Welcome! We're all up here. You can't believe all the stuff that was left behind. We've got to get it out before we can do anything."

Diego's mom appeared at the top of the staircase. She was small and pretty. She worked as a nurse. Paige liked her. Everyone liked her.

"Welcome," she said. "I'd give you the tour. But today there's no time. We've got two movers hauling stuff." She snapped her fingers. "Hey! Can you guys do us a favor? Check out the basement? We could use a report on what's down there. How much junk? Be careful. I don't think there's much light."

"Sure thing, Mom. We can use our phones." Diego held up his cellphone.

"You guys with your tech," said his mom. "Thanks. Take it slow."

It wasn't hard to find the basement door. The door was in a hallway. The hall lead to the kitchen. Diego found the light switch. Just one bulb worked. It made sense. Those bulbs had to be fourteen years old.

"Okay," Paige said. "Let's use your cell lights." She didn't want anyone to trip in the dark. They all switched on. Then they scanned the basement.

"Holy moly!" Nate said.

"You can say that again! You're going to need an army to clean this out," Ava said.

Paige took in the scene. It was a total fire hazard. There was barely room to move.

The basement was full. Papers. Tables and chairs. Chests. Tools. Clothes. Books. Old newspapers in stacks. The Bensons had left it a mess.

Ava shined her light on a giant black chest to her right. It looked like a casket. A tiny lock held it shut. "What do you think is in there?"

"I know you. You think there's a dead body," Nate said.

"No I don't. But let's open it," Ava said.

Paige looked up at Diego. "You want to? Your parents just wanted you to look around."

Ava moved toward the box. "It could be money. Don't you want to go upstairs with ten thousand bucks to show your dad, Diego? He loves money."

Paige smiled. The chances of there being money in the chest were slim. But who knew? Maybe there was something of value.

Diego seemed to think the same thing. "Sure. Let's check it out."

They moved some junk. Diego tried to open the chest with his hands. The lock held. No-go. There was so much stuff in the basement. It was easy to find something to bust the lock. He used a brick.

Wham!

The lock broke. Diego eased it from the latch. All he had to do was open the lid. He stopped.

"What if there *is* a body in it?" he asked.

"That's crazy," Nate told him. "Just do it."

Paige looked at him. "I think it's fine."

Diego opened the lid.

"Oh my God!" he screamed.

Paige retched. So did the other kids. She wasn't sure what was in the chest. But it smelled awful.

CHAPTER 2

THE BOOK

Diego gagged. This was the worst smell ever. His friends gagged too. Diego slammed the lid closed. That helped. What had been in there? He looked at Paige, not sure what to do.

"The scientist in me wants to know. What the heck was that?" she told him. "If we hold our breath, we won't smell anything." Paige always had the best ideas.

"That'll give us thirty seconds," Nate said.

"Actually, more," Diego said. "Probably

a minute. If there's something dead, we want to know. Right?"

"Right!" Ava agreed. She seemed to have made a quick recovery. "If it's a body, we can take a picture. But remember the cop shows. Don't touch anything. We can't move it either."

Diego took hold of the lid. "Okay. Here we go. On my count. Hold your breath on two. I'll open on three. One, two, three!"

He opened the lid again. The kids peered into the chest. Paige shined her light into it.

It was empty.

No. Diego saw something in there. A knife. About eight inches long with a black handle. The blade was silver. Diego ran his finger over it. The blade was sharp. He took the knife out and set it to one side. He didn't breathe again until he'd shut the lid.

"Weird," Ava said. "If the chest is empty, what made the smell?"

"Not the knife," Nate said.

"True. Knives don't stink," Paige agreed.

Diego had no idea either.

The kids took the chest out to the curb. Diego's parents were there, taking a rest. The junk pile by the curb was bigger than ever.

"How is it in the basement?" his mom asked.

Diego didn't say anything about the bad smell. He figured it was just stale air. It would take a lot of work to get the basement clean.

"It's jammed with crap," Diego said.

"The Bensons had to be hoarders. Too bad they didn't have a TV show," Ava said.

"Great," said Mr. Jones with a sigh. "More junk to deal with. These movers are fifty bucks an hour. Why did I ever buy this place?"

"Um, you wanted to torture us?" Mrs. Jones joked.

Diego got an idea. He and his friends always needed money. It was one of the reasons they'd opened that chest. Maybe they could turn the messy basement into cash. "Well, there's four of us. How about if we clean it out? We'll take out all but the biggest stuff. And you don't have to pay us fifty bucks an hour. We'll take thirty. Right, guys?"

He looked at his friends. They were nodding and grinning. None of them had jobs.

"It's a deal," Mr. Jones said. "Don't handle anything too big. I don't need any lawsuits for injured backs. "

"No problem, Dad," Diego said. "We're young. Our backs are fine."

Mr. Jones touched his lower back. He winced. "Yeah. You're young. I'm not. Don't remind me."

The kids went inside to start work. They set up a line. Diego picked out an item. He handed it to Paige. She passed it to Ava on the stairs. Ava gave it to Nate. Nate put it in a box. It was better than everyone having to climb stairs with each item.

The labor was hot and dusty. There was no A/C in the basement. Diego wiped his forehead with this hand. That was a mistake. His hands were dirty from the dust. Now his face was too.

Ava suddenly called out. "Hey, you guys! Hold it. Check this out!"

Everyone stopped and joined her. Ava held up a book.

"What have you got, Ava? A signed first edition of *Silas Marner*?" Paige joked. "I know you're dying to read that."

Ava tapped the book in her hands. "Nope. I'm totally reading this." She held it up so the others could read the title. *The Witch's Cookbook.*

"Who found this?" Ava asked.

"I did," Diego said.

"Where?"

"Um ... I'm not sure."

"Show me," Ava said. "Come on, guys. Mrs. Benson might have been a witch!"

The kids looked around for a while. Diego wasn't happy. Time was wasting. He hated to charge his dad if they weren't—

"Bingo!" Ava called. She and Paige had waded deep into the basement.

Diego and Nate made their way to the girls. The girls shined their lights on a bookcase. It was full of books about witchcraft.

Whoa! Maybe it was true. Maybe Mrs. Benson—or Mr. Benson—had been a witch. Or a demon. Or something. Nah. That was stupid. There was no such thing.

"Toss them," Diego said.

"I'll take them," Ava declared.

Diego didn't care what happened to the books. They were just more crap. "Suit yourself."

Ava grinned happily. "You never know, Diego. Someday you might want to put a spell on some-one. Like Paige. These books could come in very handy. When you do? Call me."

CHAPTER 3

UNDER THE STAIRS

Diego woke up suddenly. He blinked. Where was he? Then he heard Nate snore.

He reached for his phone to see the time. 11:15 p.m. Oh. He knew where he was. His new bedroom. In the new house. He was in bed. Nate was on an air mattress. The rest of the room was a mess.

The move-in was barely done. The kids had worked in the basement for hours. Then his parents got them pizza. Both boys had been tired. Too tired even to eat much. He and Nate had showered. They were in bed by nine. It was his earliest bedtime since third grade.

Now Diego was awake. He wasn't sleepy. In fact, he was starved. There was leftover pizza in the fridge. Cold pizza? He hated to eat it cold. But a chilled slice or two sounded pretty good. With a big glass of milk.

Time for a kitchen raid.

His new room was on the third floor. He pulled on a T-shirt to go with his shorts. Then he put on socks. He wanted to be quiet and keep his feet clean.

Diego went to the kitchen. The stairs had only creaked a little. That was good. So were the pizza and milk. He wolfed down two cheesy pieces. Okay. Much better. Now back to bed.

His trip upstairs took him past the basement door. He wasn't planning to, but he stopped. He had no idea why.

"Go to bed," he told himself.

He didn't move. It was odd. Diego had a strong feeling. He needed to go down to the basement. But he didn't want to. Nope. He started toward his room again. He got as far as the stairs. Then he stopped. He shined his cell light at the basement door. Man. It was like the basement was *calling* to him.

Diego looked up the stairs. All quiet. It wasn't like him to follow a feeling. This was more like Ava. Paige would say it was crazy. But he had a feeling there was something in the basement he had missed. Something he needed to see. It had to be now. Morning would be too late.

Five silent seconds later, he'd opened the door. Diego flipped on the light. He took a sniff. All good. No vile odor. A few more seconds passed. Then he was at the bottom of the stairs. Now what?

Diego chuckled as he shined his light around. Only a quarter of the mess had been cleared. There was so much more still to do. He told himself that was why he had come down. To see how much work was left. What he needed to do now was go back to bed. There was more to do the next day—

Hold on

There was a space under the stairs. Was that a storage room? It had a door. A latch kept it closed.

"What the heck?" he muttered. "How'd we miss that?"

Part of him wanted to open the latch. Part of him wanted to go back to bed. The part that wanted to open the door won out. He flipped the latch. It moved easily. The door swung open.

A burst of green light blinded him. Diego's hands flew to his eyes. It was like a million green lasers blasting full power. They all aimed right at his face!

CHAPTER 4

MINI-MONSTER

The green light was strong. It seemed impossible that it could get any brighter. But it did. It was like Diego had flown into a green sun. There was no heat, though. Just light so bright that—

All went black!

Diego feared he had been blinded. His hands covered his face. He'd put them there to protect his eyes. He cautiously cracked them open. There was still a green glow in the room under the stairs. But it wasn't blinding anymore. He moved his hands away. Then moved toward the light.

What he saw made him gasp.

It was a *monster*. There was a monster in the little room.

"No," Diego groaned. He slammed his eyelids shut. "No, no, no!"

He wanted to cry for his parents. Was this a dream? Was he seeing things? He opened his eyes again. Nope. There *it* was. Whatever *it* was.

It was just a few inches high. It stood on two legs with tiny-clawed feet. Black legs. Blue body. Its green-yellow head was the source of the glow. There were small ears. Two sets of bat-like wings. It had the face of a fly, with huge eyes.

It turned to stare at him. Diego felt he could not break its gaze. If he did, something bad would happen. He just had a feeling. He stared at the ugly creature. It was unlike anything he had ever seen. It was monstrous.

Should he just stand there? No. He had to do something. Diego took out his phone. The creature did not move. It just kept glowing. Diego snapped a few pictures. Then he eased the door shut. Latched it. Then he dragged a heavy chair in front of it. Now the tiny monster was trapped.

It only took a few seconds for him to get upstairs. He had already decided what to do. He went to Nate and shook him awake.

"Dude! Get up! Get. Up."

"What the—what's the matter with you? Lemme sleep, jerk!" Nate muttered.

Diego was not about to let that happen. "I have to show you something. In the basement. Now. It can't wait. Come on!"

He grabbed Nate's left arm and pulled it. With the other hand, he yanked away Nate's blanket.

"Okay, okay! Give me a sec, dude. Hand me a T-shirt. And my shoes."

Nate got out of bed.

"Thanks, man," Diego said. "You're not going to believe what I just saw."

"What were you doing in the basement?"

Diego shook his head. "Doesn't matter. Just follow me. You'll want to see this."

They went down to the basement. With Nate's help, they moved the chair away.

"If there's a bright light, shut your eyes," Diego told Nate. "It'll pass."

Nate made a face. "This better be good. Because I'm beat. I want to sleep."

"It's good. Trust me."

Should he speak up? Tell Nate what he was about to see? Diego didn't want his friend to faint. Then he decided not to tell. It was better with no preview.

"Stay quiet. No matter what you see. My folks are sleeping," Diego said. "Okay, here goes. One, two, three!"

Diego flipped up the latch. Then he pulled open the door.

He had told Nate not to scream. He was glad he did. What they saw would make any normal person scream. There was the same green light as before. Just a flash this time. It dropped back to a dull glow. Diego could see into the room.

There was not one tiny monster staring up at them.

There were *two* of them.

CHAPTER 5

STRIKE OUT

Ava had come down with a stomach bug. Paige's family went to the beach. Diego and Nate decided what to do. They chose to keep the chair in front of the door. The boys would wait for Ava and Paige. Paige was so smart. She'd know the next step.

It was a long weekend. The boys cleaned the basement. Every load took them past the room under the stairs. They didn't open it. They wanted to wait for the girls. Money was being made. But it was tough. The junk was endless. Plus, they had this big secret. Diego almost told his parents. Somehow he managed to keep his mouth shut.

Finally it was Sunday night. Diego had texted Paige. He said he had something amazing to show her. Nate had done the same with Ava. They'd decided not to send the cellphone pictures. The girls wouldn't think the creatures were real. What they saw with their own eyes? That could not be denied. All the guys said was how two things lived under the stairs. They were ugly. And they were alive.

They stood in a semicircle around the door. Paige looked skeptical. Ava was excited.

"What's the ugliest animal in the world?" Paige asked.

"Muskrat," Ava said.

"I think opossum," Paige said. "There's probably a nest."

"Opossums don't build nests indoors," Nate said.

"There's always a first time," Paige said.

Diego had a small backpack. He opened it. He had stashed four pairs of dark sunglasses in there. He gave one pair to each of his friends.

"Why these?" Paige asked. She looked puzzled by the sunglasses. "Punk rock night at Diego's house?"

Ava laughed. "Yeah. Diego's going retro."

Diego and Nate didn't laugh. Hopefully the sunglasses would block the green glow. It had been smart for Diego to bring them.

"You'll want them," Nate said. "That's all I want to say."

Paige moved next to Diego. She kept her voice low. "Should I be scared?"

"I don't know," Diego said. "You like facts? This is the strangest fact ever."

She cleared her throat. "Hold on a sec. I'll be right back."

Diego watched as Paige waded into the piles of junk behind them. She was clearly looking for something. Then she found it. It was the knife that had been in the chest.

"Just in case," she told them.

"Can we just do this?" Ava asked.

"Sunglasses on!" Diego ordered.

When everyone was ready, Diego counted off. "One, two, three."

He flung the door open. The room was dark.

"Just wait a sec," he said.

The room stayed dark. No green light. No light at all.

"What's going on?" Paige asked.

"I don't know," Diego said. "Hang tight."

Diego took off his sunglasses. He flicked on his cellphone. His flashlight lit up the room.

"What the—"

He was ready for anything ... except what he saw.

The room under the stairs was empty.

The girls erupted.

"You punked us!" Paige laughed.

"Omigod, we are such suckers!" Ava yelled. She laughed too.

Nate and Diego looked at each other. Nate shined his light into the room too. Nothing.

"Okay, you got us," Paige said with a huge grin. "Now let's go get some food."

Diego took her by the arms. "We're not punking you. I swear it. They were real." He looked over to Nate. "Right?"

His friend nodded. Nate kept quiet. His face was white.

Ava edged closer to Nate. "Nate? What did you guys see?"

Diego stepped into the space under the stairs. He shined the light around. Nothing. Where were they? It was a mystery.

He snapped his cellphone off. A flush of energy went through him. He had the answer. It was right in his hand. His phone. He'd taken pictures. All he had to do was show them to the girls. They would believe them. Would they think the photos were fake?

"Stand by. I've got pictures on my phone," he said. "Nate, tell them they're real."

"I swear it." Nate's words came from his heart.

"I swear it too," Diego said. "Okay. Let me show you guys."

He got to his photo file. He hadn't taken any other photos since Friday night. That meant the pictures should be right on top.

They weren't. He scrolled forward. He scrolled back. No pictures. Nothing at all.

Like the monsters, the photos were gone.

CHAPTER 6

THE RETURN

Diego couldn't help it. He awoke on Monday with a stupid kids' song in his head.

No more pencils
No more books
No more teacher's dirty looks!

There were just two days of school left. Monday and Tuesday. Neither day really mattered.

Monday was Field Day. There would be sports and races. Lunch would be a picnic. School would get out early. The eighth-grade dance was that night. Tuesday was another short day. It would start with breakfast on the school lawn.

The new house was looking better. Over the weekend most of the junk had been taken out. Their furniture had been moved in. Diego's room was a mess. He'd have to clean it before he went downstairs. That was a big parental rule. He had to admit he liked the new place. It was way bigger than the old house. The windows were awesome. His mom could grow flowers in the yard. The basement would be a cool hangout.

He had no more ideas about the monsters. Maybe they had mistaken animals for them. Well, it was over now. Time to get up. He swung his legs over the side of the bed and stood.

There it was. Green light.

Diego felt like he was punched in the stomach.

He knew what it was. The monster. It was back. In. His. Room.

But where?

He shielded his eyes. Looked around. There it was. Standing next to his dresser. It was bigger than the last time he'd seen it. The size of a cowboy boot. It was uglier too. Scalier. Its blue chest had scales like a fish.

The light in the room dimmed to a dull glow. Then the monster spoke to him.

"Help me!"

Diego shook his head. No. There was no way. He had heard the creature. In English. But there had been no sound. How was that even possible? He had read about telepathy. That was where two people could talk with no words. He and his buds had tried it. They had all failed. Ava still believed in it. Diego had thought she was nuts. Maybe proof was now in his room.

"Did you talk to me?" Diego asked. He kept

his voice down. He didn't want his parents to wander in.

"Help me!" the monster repeated. Again there was no sound. "Help me. I can help you!"

There was a huge burst of green light. It flashed like a strobe. Diego started to feel sick. The light dimmed back to dull green. Then it went out.

His room was now spotless. Whoa! How had that happened? Who had done that?

It was a situation that defied logic. Still, Diego asked a logical question.

"What do you want?"

It wanted food. And water. That was why it had come out from under the stairs. It wanted to return to the closet. It was safe in there. But it did not want to starve.

Diego found food. He sneaked it to the basement. A peanut butter and jelly sandwich. He got a big bowl of water too. He took it to the closet. The creature was already back. It must have gotten there through the air vents.

The monster ate. Drank. And talked a little. It didn't have much to say.

How often did it need to eat? Once a day.

Where had it come from? The monster had no idea.

Did it have parents? The creature did not understand the word.

Did the monster have a name? Again, it had no clue.

What would happen to it in the days and weeks ahead? No info.

Then Diego asked what had happened to the other little monster. Here, the monster said one word. It wasn't angry. It wasn't mad. It was just a fact.

"Gone."

Diego winced. He had the oddest feeling to this news. He felt sad.

CHAPTER 7

FIELD DAY

Two more days!" Paige told Diego. "And tonight is the dance. I'm so psyched. It's going to be such a great summer. It's official. I'm going to camp for four weeks. My parents just signed me up. I leave in a week. It's up in Maine. Rocket camp. We're going to build rockets. Then I'm coming home. We can hang out then. It's going to be a blast."

An hour later Diego was at school. Field Day was about to start. He was with Paige. Ava was still stuck in homeroom. Nate hadn't showed up at all.

Diego had texted him. He heard nothing back. He wondered if Nate had gotten Ava's stomach bug. That would suck.

"Yeah, it's going to be awesome," Diego told Paige.

Paige was all excited. She kept talking about rocket camp. There would be people there from NASA. "Maybe I'll build a rocket to go to Europa. You know, a moon of Jupiter. Not this summer. But one day. That place has frozen water. Maybe even life."

She kept talking. Diego hardly listened. His mind was at home. In the basement. Under the stairs with the monster. He still marveled at the morning. That he and the monster could talk with no words was amazing. They had a bond. He didn't know what the monster was. It might not even be of this world. He had to protect it.

At some point the monster might even make him rich. He didn't want to scare it. The other monster had gone away. It had to be dead. Diego didn't want that to happen to his monster too.

Wow! He realized he had just called it "his monster." That's what it felt like. It felt almost like it was part of him.

"Diego? Diego?"

He looked at Paige. He had totally zoned out.

"Yeah?"

Paige glared at him. "What did I just say?"

Diego squirmed. Paige hated it when people got distracted. Kids did it with phones. Paige always called them out. It was one of the reasons she said she liked him. She never felt overlooked. Diego knew she bragged to other girls how Diego always listened.

Well, he had just overlooked her. And she'd nailed him.

At least he didn't lie.

"I don't know. I was thinking," he said.

At the other end of the field, kids gathered

around the gym coach. He was up on a ladder with a megaphone. The day would start with a tug-of-war. The coach was about to say which kid was on what team. Diego knew he and Paige didn't have much time. Where was Nate? He checked his phone. It hadn't sounded. Did he miss a text? Nope.

"Expecting a text from a new girl?" Paige asked. "Is she who you were thinking about?"

Diego shook his head. "No. I thought maybe Nate would have texted me. He's late. Maybe he's cutting."

Paige seemed to soften a bit. "I don't care about Nate. I care about you. If it's not a new girl whose butt I need to kick? Then what is it? What were you thinking about?"

Diego was about to blame it on having a hard time sleeping at the new house. It was partly true. Then the coach blew his whistle. He divided the kids into teams by their classes. Other teachers set out a hundred-foot rope.

The tug-of-war would be across a sandy area. When the first kid got pulled into the area, the contest would be over. Diego and Paige found themselves on different sides. The game was about to start. Just then Nate came running over to join Diego's team.

"Where've you been?" Diego asked.

"You won't believe it," Nate said.

"Try me. My morning's been sick!"

Nate leaned close. He didn't want any of the other kids to hear. "When I woke up, there was a monster in my room! It begged me for food and water. I've got it out in the shed. Know what it said to me?"

Diego nodded. "Yup. I think I do. It said if you would help it, it would help you."

"How do you know that?" Nate asked.

"I've got a monster too."

CHAPTER 8

THE DANCE

Ava brushed Paige's hair. The two girls were at Paige's house. They'd decided to dress and go together to the dance.

Paige's mom had bought her a little black dress. It was a reward for how well she had done in school that year. It had a sweetheart neckline. There was lace at the bottom. It looked great with her blonde hair.

Ava had a green cami and black skirt. The

cami was silk. In her heels she would be nearly as tall as Paige.

They had been looking forward to this dance. Ava would hang with Nate. Paige would be with Diego. Once, Paige was sure Diego would kiss her at this dance. Now? She didn't know. He was acting odd.

"I'm still thinking about the guys," Paige said. Ava worked on her hair.

"That they were total jerks today? Yeah, I kind of got that," Ava said with sniff.

"Any idea why?"

"Maybe Diego's house put a spell on them? Beats me." Ava held up a mirror. "Here. Look. You're perfect."

Paige took a quick peek. Then she grinned at her friend. She loved Ava's outfit. "No, you're perfect. That outfit is killer. Every boy is going to want you. Anyway, I would have thought you believed it was some woo-woo thing. After those books you took home."

Ava shook her head. Paige had put Ava's dark hair into a French braid. It looked amazing against her cami. "Nope. I didn't use those books to put spells on them. I'm no witch. They're just fun to read."

Paige moved to the closet to find her shoes. It was almost seven thirty. Time to head out. "Well, then. There's just one answer."

"Which is?" Ava had her compact out. She checked her makeup.

"Hormones."

Her delivery was deadpan. It took Ava a second before she cracked up. Then Paige laughed too. It felt good. She decided to give the boys the benefit of the doubt. Maybe it was puberty. But if they screwed up again? There'd be a lot of other guys happy to take their place. The dance was the perfect spot to meet some.

Paige and Ava sat together at a table near the deejay. He was taking a break. The music was quieter. The band shell area was packed with kids. Everyone had come.

There were burgers and franks to eat. Plus plenty of cold drinks. There was a dance floor. Tables and chairs. Lights were strung overhead. Big fans kept everything cool. It was a mild night.

Perfect for a dance.

Perfect for a first kiss.

The only problems were Diego and Nate. They'd shown up. But they'd spent most of the night in deep talk. It was like they didn't want to include the girls at all. When Ava and Paige had tried to join them, the guys had clammed up.

"I say we give them a chance," Paige told Ava.

Ava frowned. "I'm not into being dissed."

"Hello, ladies."

Paige looked up. There stood Trevor Freeman and Mike Walls. They played on the school soccer team. They were two fine guys. They also were decent. Neither had talked to Paige or Ava before. They knew the girls had boyfriends. Everyone did.

"Hey, Trevor. Hey, Mike," Paige said. She tried to be nice.

"Where are your guys?" Trevor asked. "We thought you'd be with them."

Ava laughed. Her voice was cold. "So did we."

Mike slid a little closer. "Can we ask you to dance? Would you get out there with us?"

"Maybe," Paige said.

She looked past Trevor and Mike. There were Diego and Nate. They were about twenty feet away. Once again they were in heavy-duty talk mode. She waved at Diego for a long time. He had to notice her, right? Didn't he see the two hot guys?

Finally Diego saw her. So did Nate. They seemed to take in the moment. Then Diego waved. He started talking to Nate again. The girls were forgotten.

Paige hated to be ignored. She gritted her teeth. As she did, the music started. She got to her feet. Then she took Trevor's arm.

"Come on," she told him. "Let's dance."

CHAPTER 9

LAST DAY

It was Tuesday morning. The last day of school. Diego had set the alarm for six. He'd told his mom he would go to Nate's for breakfast. Nate had said he would go to Diego's. Hopefully the parents would not check in.

Diego knew he'd been a jerk at the dance. But he and Nate had to figure things out. Show up and be jerks. It was better than not to show up at all. They would explain to the girls later. Maybe they would get it. Maybe they wouldn't. It was out of his hands.

Meanwhile, there was something big they had to do. Today was the morning to do it.

The first thing to do was bring the creature food. The monster seemed to like peanut butter.

After Diego dressed, he went downstairs. He found a big box. Then he filled the box with food and water. He figured that would hold the monster for a while. He brought the box to the basement. Then took the top off. The monster seemed to sense that he was there.

"Hungry!" Diego could hear its voice in his head.

"I'm here," Diego said aloud. "Relax."

He opened the door. Green light glowed around the creature's head. It had grown a little bigger and a lot uglier. Its eyes were like a fly's. More scales had sprouted on its skin. The feet had more claws. The arms had big talons. Diego felt himself coming under the creature's spell.

"Hungry!" the monster repeated.

Diego put the box on the ground. The monster

jumped into it. It began to munch. The peanut butter was gobbled up. Diego watched in sick amazement. He loved this monster. Then he closed his eyes. He thought of Paige. He knew what he had to do next.

Like a flash, he slammed a lid on top of the box. The monster was eating greedily. It seemed not to notice. The next step was to tape the box shut. Last night he'd put a roll of duct tape by the door. Five seconds later he was done.

He sent a text to Nate.

DIEGO: (Done. U?)

Nate had done the same thing. At least that is what Diego hoped.

The text from Nate came back right away.

NATE: (Yep!)

It was time to get into gear. He texted Nate one more time.

DIEGO: (C u at the dump.)

NATE: (Can't get there fast enough!)

The town dump was not far from school. Diego and Nate planned to bike to school when their task was done. The dump was mostly deserted. The only thing moving was a bulldozer. It was filling a pit with garbage. The air smelled gross. Like rotted food.

Diego got there first. Nate came soon after. They'd tied their boxes to the back of their bikes. Diego's monster had figured out they were on the move about halfway to the dump.

"Let me out! Let me out! Out, out, out!" it screamed.

It was hard to ignore. The monster had a strong hold on his heart. Same thing with Nate. The boys were ready for that. They'd each worn earbuds. They cranked up the music as they rode. It was not exactly safe. But it drowned out the monsters.

At the dump they put down the boxes. Then they moved away to talk. They could see the boxes wiggle. The monsters wanted to be free.

"Maybe we should let them go," Nate said. "Out here. It's safe."

Diego shook his head. They'd made a plan to get their lives back. They should stick to it.

"I don't know what they are. I just want them dead. Don't you?"

Nate nodded. "You know it."

"I don't care if they can do magic. I don't care if they can turn this dump into gold. They're ruining our lives. Paige and Ava hate us."

"Then let's do it."

"No changes. No wussing out," Diego said. "Stick to the plan. Got it?"

They fist-bumped. Then Diego counted down. "Three. Two. One."

The boys ran toward the boxes. They grabbed them without stopping. As they did, the monsters started up again.

"Let us out!"

"Let us go!"

"We're going to get you!"

"Let us go!"

The boys didn't listen. They kept running. The pit was fifty yards away. They came to the edge. Then they threw their boxes as far as they could. The boxes tumbled to the bottom. A few moments later, the bulldozer had pushed a ton of trash over them. The boxes were gone. The monsters were buried.

It was over.

CHAPTER 10

MAKING IT RIGHT

Students sat on the lawn. Teachers always made breakfast for everyone. It was a last-day-of-school tradition for the eighth graders. Paige and Ava got there early. They'd had a good time dancing with Mike and Trevor. Those guys were fun. They had agreed to meet on the lawn. It would be another chance to hang out before the summer.

Paige still looked for Diego and Nate when she got there. She didn't see them. It did not surprise her.

All around the lawn, kids were laughing. They were eating and having a great time. Middle school had been fun. But this was the end. When the bell rang at noon, they would be ninth graders. On to high school. It was like the gate to life. Cars. College. The real world.

Paige couldn't wait. She wanted a shiny car. It didn't have to be new. It just had to be shiny. She wanted great grades. She wanted a math degree at a top college. And she wanted a boyfriend she could trust.

Paige felt bad about Diego. She felt bad for Ava too. Nate had let her down. But in a way, Paige was happy. She was a girl who wanted the truth. This was the truth. All the data she needed was right there on the lawn. She was there. Ava was there. Mike and Trevor were there. She saw them by the flagpole. But Diego and Nate were gone. Those guys were showing their true colors. They were not the colors Paige wanted to see.

Trevor and Mike found Paige and Ava as they headed to the food line.

"Hey," Mike said. "We're pumped we could hang out last night."

Ava grinned. "We had a great time too."

Trevor cleared his throat. "You know, my older brother has a car. And he loves to drive. I bet if I asked, he'd take us to Six Flags tomorrow. If it's okay with your folks. But I don't see why it wouldn't be. Oh! He's got a friend who works there. We may get passes."

"No standing in line. Ever," Mike said. "What do you think?"

Six Flags. An actual date. Paige didn't like amusement parks all that much. The big rides made her feel sick. But Ava loved Six Flags. She went as much as she could. Paige would do it for Ava. All she'd have to do was get her parents okay—

That idea stopped her. As far as her parents knew, her boyfriend was Diego. What would they say to her wanting to go to Six Flags with a new boy? Some parents didn't care about their kids' social lives. Those were not Paige's parents. They knew Diego. They liked him. They'd have a ton of questions. There'd be grilling about the guy driving the car. They'd want to talk to Trevor's parents. It would become a whole thing.

"So?" Trevor asked. "What do you say? We'll show you ladies a good time. Promise."

Ava was nodding yes. Paige wasn't ready to say yes just yet. She wanted to think about it. She was just about to say so. But then she spotted Diego and Nate. They had just come onto the lawn.

Whoa! They each held a bunch of flowers.

Diego spotted Paige. He waved shyly. What could she do? She waved back.

Diego and Nate started toward them. Paige spoke quickly to Trevor and Mike. "We'll let you know," she said.

Then she turned to Ava. She'd also seen the guys. "We need to go," Paige said.

They met Diego and Nate near the flagpole. Each boy blushed as he gave his flowers to his girlfriend. Paige loved the white roses. They were the flower of friendship. Ava liked daffodils. They made her think of springtime.

"We're sorry," Diego told Ava.

"More than sorry," Nate added.

Diego bit his lower lip. "We've acted like idiots for the last few days. It will never happen again. We took care of the problem. We did it for you two."

Ava stared at Nate. "Was it a girl?"

"No!" Nate said. "It has nothing to do with any girl. Not for me. Not for Diego. We swear it."

Paige and Ava shared a look. Could they trust them? What the heck had happened anyway?

"Okay," Paige said. "It's over. Tell us the whole truth."

"You'll never believe it," Diego said.

Paige put a hand gently on Diego's arm. "Let's get some food. Then you can tell us."

CHAPTER 11

BOY CAVE

School's out for summer!

Diego had a fun time planned. In July he would visit family in Mexico. In August he would go to his aunt's in Texas. She was a teacher. There would be a lot of prep for high school. Diego didn't mind that. He wanted to be a PT when he grew up. His aunt could help him get there.

Diego was not as smart as Paige. He knew he had to work harder. For the rest of June, Diego was home free. His parents would even let him sleep late. There were plenty of chores to do, though.

The day after school was a trip to Six Flags. The trip had been the girls' idea. That had surprised Diego. Paige hated thrill parks. They made her afraid. She said people needed to do things that scared them. That would make them less afraid. His mom drove them there. They went on all the rides. Even the death-drop ones. No one got sick. They even did the biggest coaster twice.

After that, they came back to Diego's house. His parents had a surprise. The basement was finished. Most of the junk was gone. Just a few boxes were left. The floor was washed. A rug was down. There was a big-screen TV, couch, and beanbag chairs. There was even a small fridge with drinks.

His parents said this could be Diego's hang-out. Diego hadn't kissed his father and mother in a long time. He kissed them when he heard that. He also said a silent thank you to himself and Nate.

Thank God they had taken care of the monsters. What if his parents had found them? What a nightmare that would have been.

It was nine o'clock that night. The friends were eating take-out Chinese. They ate it straight from the cartons. They were watching *Edward Scissorhands* for the tenth time. Diego's parents were down the street at some new friends' place. Diego sat next to Paige on the couch. Their legs were touching. Paige turned to Nate and Ava.

"I'm getting bored. Is it okay if Diego and I go outside for a bit?"

Ava smiled. Diego understood why. This was Paige's way of giving Ava and Nate some private time. It also meant he would have some private time with Paige. It was a win-win.

Ava and Nate had no problem with the idea. Paige and Diego went out back. There was a swing under the pine tree. They sat and looked at the sky. The moon had just risen. It was huge.

"That's just our eyes playing tricks on us,"

Paige said. "The moon is no bigger in the sky now than it is any other time."

"Really?" Diego didn't know that. "It looks bigger."

"Really. You can cut a circle of paper. Hold it up to the moon. Then put it over the moon later. You'll see. It's the same size."

"Huh. I always thought it looked bigger. Maybe because the air is thicker. Or something," Diego said.

"Nice idea. Wrong idea. Sort of like that monster of yours," Paige said lightly. "Which I am sure was kind of a trick. Like, you saw one thing. Then figured it was another. Or something."

Diego was happy she wasn't angry with him anymore. It mattered. He didn't want what happened with the monster to get between them. At the same time, he knew what he'd seen was real. True, he hadn't touched it. But he had seen it. Heard it. Fed it. Watched it eat.

"Paige, I don't know what I saw. What we saw. What it was. What they were. But we saw something."

Paige frowned. "That's what you told me. I know you, Diego. Something *did* happen to you. You changed. So did Nate. But what you're saying about a monster? Two monsters? That's just crazy. I can't accept that. So let's just forget it."

Diego paced around a bit. He tried to think of some way to explain it better. Not that it mattered much. The monsters were long dead. They were under a ton of garbage at the dump. Then he got an idea. He didn't have a picture. Maybe he could do the next best thing.

"How about if I draw what I saw for you?"

Paige raised her eyebrows. "Okay. I'd like that. It will help me to understand."

Diego told Paige to wait for him on the porch. There was a lot of light there for drawing. In fact, he walked her there. He needed to go to his room.

His sketch pad and colored pencils and other art supplies were in his closet.

"You good here for a minute?" Diego asked her.

Paige nodded. "Sure. Why wouldn't I be? Unless you're afraid I'll be eaten by monsters." She settled down onto a bench.

CHAPTER 12

KISSED

Paige heard the door creak. Her stomach flip-flopped. It was safe on the porch. She told herself to calm down. There was no such thing as monsters. It was either Diego, Ava, or Nate. Probably Diego. He'd only had to go to his room for his art supplies.

"Diego? Is that you?"

Nothing.

Panic struck. She jumped to her feet and spun around. Just then, Diego stepped onto the porch. He had a sketch pad under his right arm. In his right hand was an art supply box. It was actually an old fishing tackle box.

"Hi," he said. "Everything okay?"

"Didn't you hear me call your name?" The words came out more upset than she wanted.

"Um, no," Diego said.

Huh. Well, that was a good reason. Paige liked good reasons. She was mad that she'd lost her head for a moment.

"So," she said. She patted the seat next to her. "Let's see you draw a monster."

He put the pad on his lap. Then he opened his tackle box. Out came blue, black, green, red, and yellow pencils. He gave these to Paige to hold. Then he took the blue one from her.

"You have to remember, there were two monsters," he said. "But I'm only drawing one."

She had seen Diego draw before. He had a system. First he stared at the blank page. Then he closed his eyes. He'd told her that when he did this, he was drawing in his head. It was how he planned his lines. When he put pencil to paper, the picture always came fast. He was as good at art as she was at math.

This time, though, he didn't do his usual prep. He just drew. The legs were black. The body was blue. The wings were wide. The face was ugly. It was a mix of green and yellow. The eyes were like those of a fly.

Her eyes grew wide as he drew. "I know this thing."

"What?" Diego was shocked. "You've seen one too?"

Paige shook her head. "Nope. But I've seen it in books. Stories."

He didn't look up. Diego kept drawing. "What story?"

"A writer from a long time ago. He wrote scary stories. A lot of them had monsters."

Diego took the green pencil. He used it

to shade the face. Then he put some green light around the head. "I don't read scary stories. Did I tell you that they talked to us?"

Paige made a joke. "In French?"

"No, not in French. Without words. I could hear what it said in my head. Nate too. Like it had ESP. Ava would have loved that." He blended a few more colors on the body. Paige could make out a scaled chest. "Okay. That's it." He handed her the pad. "They're about a foot and half high. Double wings. That's what we saw."

Paige stared at the pad. Again she thought about the old horror stories. The drawing was amazing. The monster was ugly. But it was also beautiful. She knew monsters were not real. At the same time, if there was one? She wished she could have seen it.

"I'm sorry I wasn't there with you," she said.

"Really? You don't think I made the whole thing up?"

Paige shook her head. "Not so much. Your picture is too good. It's too detailed. I don't know where this came from. It doesn't make sense. Whatever you saw, Diego? I wish I had seen it too."

Diego laughed. "You'd probably want to cut it open and look at its guts."

"That too."

They both laughed.

"Thanks for doing the drawing for me," Paige said. "That helps a lot. So will this."

She did it on impulse. It was unplanned. But it was the right thing to do. She leaned over and kissed him for the first time.

He kissed her back.

CHAPTER 13

MISSING

Diego was flying. It had been his first kiss. It was a great one too. Maybe there could be more. He and Paige had a summer ahead of them. He had to treat her well. Care for her. Not overlook her. It would not be hard. She was a great girl. He had overlooked her once. She had almost dropped him. If he were a girl, he would have dropped him too.

Never again.

He found his sketch pad and tore off the

picture of the monster. Then he folded it up and gave it to her.

She raised her eyebrows. "What am I supposed to do with this? Frame it above my bed?"

"Nope. Frame the next one. I'm going to draw you."

The light on the porch was strong enough for Diego to see Paige blush. "You'd draw me?"

"Yes," he said.

"That's … I'd like that."

"Is everything okay?"

Paige smiled. "I like that idea. Let's pick a day for it. But not now. We'd better go back to the basement. Don't you think?"

Diego nodded. They'd been away for a while. He didn't want his parents to come home and find them alone on the porch. Not that they were doing anything bad. But his folks weren't born yesterday. He wanted them to trust him.

"Okay. How about in the morning for the

drawing? At the park? By the band shell. I've been there then. The light is great."

She kissed his right cheek. "I'd like that. A lot. Let's go inside."

In they went.

They were about to go down to the basement. "We'd better make some noise," Diego said. He thought that Nate and Ava might be kissing too. He didn't want them to feel like they'd been busted.

"Good idea," Paige said.

That's what they did. But they didn't need to. Their friends were gone.

Diego and Paige searched everywhere. Nate and Ava were not in the basement. They weren't upstairs. They hadn't gone out back. Paige even took a run around the block to see if they'd gone for a walk. Nothing.

"They didn't text you, did they?" Diego asked.

"Negative. Hey. Maybe they left a note."

The two of them hustled back to the basement. No note. Nothing on the couch. Nothing on the floor. Diego checked his phone to see if maybe a text had come in. Like Paige, there was nothing.

"What do we do?" Paige asked.

"Call my folks. We need their help." Diego scanned the basement. Everything looked normal. He saw the long knife that had been in the chest that first day. It was still on top of one of the boxes. Huh? His parents must have set it down. It needed to be stashed someplace safe. But not now. Now they needed to find their friends.

"I'll call my parents," he said. "You call ..."

His voice trailed off.

"What?" Paige asked.

His eyes were fixed on the space under the basement stairs. The door was closed. Without explaining, he tugged Paige toward the staircase.

"What?"

"Under the stairs. It's the one place we haven't looked."

He yanked on the door. It opened easily.

He was blinded by a burst of green light. So was Paige. Screams filled their ears.

"Argh!"

CHAPTER 14

THEY'RE BACK

It wasn't the monsters.

The green lights went out. They had come from two cellphones. The screams had been human. Nate and Ava emerged from the small space. They were in tears. The two put their cellphones into their pockets. Then they pointed at Diego and Paige. Those two just stood there, mouths open.

"Omigod!" Ava laughed. "We punked you!"

"Woot, woot, woot!" Nate pointed at Diego. Then he danced around him.

"We should have taken pictures. You guys turned white. It would be the tweet of all time!" Ava and Nate were holding each other up, laughing so hard.

Diego just stood there and grinned. He couldn't remember the last time he had been punked. Maybe it was in sixth grade. A bunch of kids in his class had told him they had a copy of a test. They did, but it was a test they'd made up. He'd learned his lesson. Do. Not. Cheat. Now there seemed to be another lesson to learn.

Paige had been punked too. She was smiling like Diego.

"Okay. I have something to say," Paige said.

Everyone got quiet.

"When that green light came on?" Paige said. "I was scared. But part of me was glad. Because it would mean that Diego and Nate were telling the truth. Diego drew me a picture of the monster. It looks real. I don't know what to think."

Diego didn't feel like yet another talk about

the monsters. He'd just been goofed on because of them. He'd rather think about his first kiss with Paige. A second kiss would be great. He had an idea how to make that happen.

"It's a nice night," he told his friends. "Maybe you guys want to hang out on the front porch. We can take some food. There's fruit in the kitchen."

"That's a great idea!" Paige said.

Diego beamed. That was the right answer. Maybe there would be another kiss.

They picked up their mess. All the food cartons went into the trash. Then they started up the basement stairs. When they were nearly at the top, the door opened on its own.

Diego's eyes flew to Paige's face. The light pouring down the stairs was so intense. He could feel his pupils contracting into pinpricks. Behind him, he could hear Ava screaming. Paige and Nate were screaming too.

"Oh no!" Diego cried.

"It's them!" Nate yelled. "We need to run!"

"There's only one way out!" Ava shouted back.

Diego was stunned. When they had brought the monsters to the dump, they could fit in boxes. Not now. They were huge. They were the size of football linemen. Their legs were blacker than ever. The body was dark blue and scaly. Their necks were ringed. Their heads yellow-and-green striped. Those fly-like eyes were now the size of Frisbees. Each mass pulsed. The arm talons were huge. When they spread their wings, they went from wall to wall.

"How'd they get so huge?" Diego yelled.

"I don't know!" Nate hollered back.

Paige knew. "You took them to the dump. It's full of rotted food. They got out of their boxes. Then they ate like pigs!"

"How'd they get here? How come no one saw them?" Nate asked.

Again, Paige answered. "You guys are idiots. They have wings. They flew."

The monsters leaped downstairs until they stood at the bottom of the staircase. As they did, the kids backed up into the room. Diego knew in his gut that any sudden move on their part could mean instant death. He didn't dare go for his cellphone.

One of the monsters screamed. It was the worst thing Diego had ever heard in his life. He covered Paige's ears. Then that monster spoke. It didn't move its thick lips. But all the kids heard it in their heads.

"Diego! What did you do to us? Why did you want to kill us? We came to help you! We love you and Nate. You meant to kill us! Why? Why? *Why*?"

One monster's eyes were on Diego. The other's were on Nate. Diego knew he had to say something. But what? He stepped forward.

"Look. It's my fault," he said softly. "If it weren't for me, you would never have met Nate. So whatever you're here to do, do it to me. Leave my friends alone. Okay?"

Then Diego turned to his friends. "Go. Save

yourselves. Please." He locked eyes with Paige. "Please. Do it for me."

The monster yelled again. "You didn't answer me! Why?"

They attacked him.

Green light filled the room. They tried to smother him in their massive bodies. Diego screamed and fought back. He punched the monsters in their guts. The blows seemed useless. The monsters cut at his skin. Their talons were like razors. His shirt was ripped and torn. Blood dripped from Diego's chest. It ran like a red river.

CHAPTER 15

DEATH IN THE BASEMENT

Paige looked to Ava and Nate. They cowered near the couch. Paige knew the smart thing to do would be to run upstairs. Save their lives. No! She had to help her friend. *Boyfriend.*

With a wild scream, she rushed at the creatures. Her arms wrapped around one of their necks. The beast tried to throw her off. She hung on. As she did, Nate and Ava went at the other one. They tore its wings from its body.

Both creatures screamed. They left Diego

alone for a moment. Paige kept the chokehold on. It was no use. The other monster flung Nate and Ava across the room. They smashed into the wall.

Diego tried to help Paige. A monster slashed at him. He fell back. Then Paige felt herself pushed down. The power of the monster was intense. Her head struck the floor with a giant thud. Paige's head bounced once, then rested on the floor. Paige felt the world fade to black. She forced her eyes open and slapped her own face to stay awake. Then her mind cleared. She pushed herself up to her feet.

Diego's cries of pain rose. The monsters were on both sides of him. They had locked their arms around his torso. They were squeezing the breath from him. His cries faded. He had to be dying.

Diego had wanted Paige to save herself. Paige would not let her friend die. She looked around for something—anything!—to use as a weapon. She saw the knife. It was still on top of some boxes.

She had no idea if it would pierce the scaly skin of the monsters. But it might.

She grabbed it. Ava and Nate saw what she was doing. They looked for weapons too.

Paige remembered Diego's art box. There had to be stuff in there. She shouted for them to go to it. They did. Ava found a razor blade. Nate grabbed a sharp pen. Then Paige ran at one of the monsters. As it turned to her, she thrust the knife into its gut. It bellowed in pain, then raked at her face with its talons.

Monster blood spilled to the concrete floor. It stank. It was the same vile odor that had been in the locked chest. Paige found herself gagging. But she turned her attention to the second monster. It had let Diego fall to the floor. He was facedown. Blood covered his body. Paige didn't know if he was alive or dead.

They had to kill these two things. Or they would all be dead.

Ava and Nate jabbed at the creatures with their weapons. Paige danced in and out with the knife. She cut a monster across its throat. The smell was awful.

Thud!

The creature fell to the floor next to Diego.

One was left.

It moved toward Paige, arms spread. Its arms were far longer than hers. If she tried to stab it, it would slash her. She backed away. So did Nate and Ava. The monster faced each of them in turn. The stench in the room was brutal.

The monster lunged at Paige.

She did the only thing she could. She had never thrown a knife in her life. Still, she flung it at the creature. The range was close. There was time for the knife to rotate maybe one time. It stuck in the monster's gut just as its talons reached her neck. The monster screamed. Its talons reached for the knife. But it had no way to grab it. The talons could not hold on. The creature staggered. Then it fell to the floor.

It was dead.

The stench was the worst yet.

Paige didn't waste a second. She ran to Diego. So did Ava and Nate. She put a finger on his wrist. There was a pulse. Barely.

"Call 911! Now!" she yelled.

There was no need. What happened next made no sense. It was impossible. Before her eyes, she watched Diego's wounds bind up. The blood literally flowed back inside him. His torn clothing repaired itself. His bruised skin returned to normal. Then he sat up.

"Hi," he said. It was as simple as if he had just seen Paige at school.

Paige flung herself into his arms. "Omigod. Thank you! You're alive! Do you remember?"

He nodded. "I do. Yes. At least until they

were squeezing me. What happened? Where are the monsters? What happened to them? It stinks in here."

"They're dead. I killed them. They're behind me."

Diego looked puzzled. "No they're not."

Paige turned around.

The monsters' bodies were gone. The blood was gone. Even the mess was gone. The basement was back to normal. Only the stench remained. Then it was gone too.

Paige got to her feet like a zombie. She moved toward the knife that was still on the floor. Nate and Ava told Diego what had happened. They said Paige saved his life.

Paige picked up the knife. It was all coming clear about the Bensons. There must have been a small monster in the chest. It had killed most of the family. One of them must have stabbed it. Then it died. That was the reason for the bad odor. The monster had disappeared, just like the monsters here. As for the padlock, who knew? Someone else might have put it on the chest. Maybe a relative.

What if there were other monsters? No. That didn't make sense. They would be here by now, Paige thought.

There was a knock at the basement door. Then it opened. Mr. Jones came halfway down the stairs. "Hi, guys, we're back. All good?"

Diego cleared his throat. "Yeah, we're great. All good."

Mr. Jones nodded. "Man, there was a funky smell upstairs. Thought maybe it came from down here."

"Maybe it's the septic tank," Paige said. She knew very well what Mr. Jones had smelled.

"Maybe," Mr. Jones agreed. "Anyway, I'm outta here. Have fun. Diego, curfew is at ten."

He left. The kids looked at each other.

"Wanna play cards?" Diego asked.

They laughed at that.

"I think I'm going to head home," Ava said.

"Let me walk you," Nate told her.

"I'd better go home too. It's been … interesting," Paige told Diego.

Five minutes later, Ava and Nate had gone. Diego and Paige lingered on the porch.

"Some night," Paige said.

"Thank you. For saving my life." Diego's voice was low.

"Thank you. For being willing to die for us," Paige answered.

Diego smiled slyly. "Want to play cards?"

Paige pointed to the sky. "Look at the moon."

They looked. The full moon was higher in the sky. The ruddy yellow of moonrise had given way to a white orb. It was so bright that Paige wondered if she could read by it. Beyond the moon was the universe. It was full of mysteries.

"There's a lot we still don't know," she said. "I want to go out there. Someday."

"Here's what I know," Diego said.

He kissed her. She kissed him back. For the moment someday would have to wait.

WANT TO KEEP READING?

9781680211092

Turn the page for a sneak
peek at another book in the
White Lightning series:

REBEL

CHAPTER 1

TO SEE THE WORLD

Dear Patrick,

Thank you for your letter. Your family and home in America sound very nice. I would like to visit your country one day. I would especially like to see Disneyland. And I would like to meet Mickey Mouse.

You asked me to describe my home and myself. I live in a small village in Africa. It is the dry season now. It is very dusty. In a few months the rains will come. Then the ground will turn muddy. The grass will grow. I don't like mud. But we need the grass for our cattle.

I have a mother and father. I also have three younger sisters. I have many aunts, uncles, and cousins. Two of my grandparents live in our village. Our house is round. Our roof is made of reeds. The school is square. It has a blue metal roof. It is loud when the rain falls.

My best friend is Jojo. We play soccer. Only we call it football. Do you like football? I like it. I would play it all day long if I could. But I like school too. I like learning about the world. My favorite subject is geography. I want to become a teacher one day.

I am looking forward to being your pen pal.

Sincerely,
Koji

I set my pencil down. Most of my classmates are still writing. Including Jojo. Maybe I should write more. But I read over my letter. Decide it's enough. I hope Patrick writes back. I want to learn more about his life halfway around the world. I pick up my pencil again. Write a note at the bottom of the page.

Please tell me more about your life in America.

There. Now it's enough.

"Time to finish," Mr. Wek says.

Pencils hit the desks.

"Put your letters in the envelopes you addressed," he says. "Pass them to me. I will see that they get mailed."

I watch my letter. It goes hand over hand to the front of the classroom. The beginning of its long journey. I wonder how it will travel. By plane? By boat? I wish I could travel with it.

"Get out your math books," Mr. Wek says.

A few students groan. Jojo too. They don't like math. I don't mind it. I'm going to be a teacher. So I will need to know many things.

It's the end of the day. I'm restless. Want to go outside. But I try to sit still. Don't want a scolding from Mr. Wek. Finally he says, "History exam tomorrow. You may go."

Jojo and I are the first out of our seats. "Race you home," he says.

The village is a mile north. We run the whole way. I sprint at the end. But he still beats me.

"Hah! I won!" he shouts. He throws his hands in the air. Like he's a big champion.

"I'll beat you one of these days," I tell him.

"No you won't," he says. "My legs will always be longer than yours."

"Maybe. But I'm a better footballer."

He laughs. "You are not."

"Am so." I run to our hut. Grab my football. But I don't leave quickly enough.

"Koji!" my mother says. "Change out of your

uniform. And put down that ball. I need you to fetch water."

I groan. "Why can't Onaya do it?"

"Because she's helping me cook. Go on."

I quickly change out of my yellow uniform. I grab the plastic water jug. Carry it outside.

Jojo is playing football with his brothers. I sneak up behind him. Steal the ball out from under his foot. "Hey!" he shouts.

"See?" I laugh. "I told you I'm better!"

I play with them for a few minutes. I'm still holding the water jug. I'm tempted to set it down. And really play. But I need to get going or Mama will be angry.

The pump is at the other end of the village. I pass the village leader's hut. He sits outside. A number of men sit around him. My father's there. I'm surprised to see Papa here. He's usually out with our cattle.

I leave the path. Step closer to them. One man points south. Another points west. They speak in hushed and hurried voices. The one word I hear sends a chill through me. "Soldiers."

Papa spies me. Shoos me away.